Freddie and Flossie and the Easter Egg Hunt

Visit us at www.abdopub.com

Spotlight, a division of ABDO Publishing Company, is a school and library distributor of high quality reinforced library bound editions.

Library bound edition © 2006

Library of Congress Cataloging-in-Publication Data

Hope, Laura Lee.
Freddie and Flossie and the Easter egg hunt / by Laura Lee Hope; illustrated by Maggie Downer.—1st ed.
p. cm.—(Bobbsey twins) (Ready-to-Read)
Summary: Twins Freddie and Flossie have a hard time finding Easter eggs when their dog Snap is around.
ISBN-13: 978-1-4169-1029-9
ISBN-10: 1-4169-1029-8
[1. Twins—Fiction. 2. Brothers and sisters—Fiction. 3. Easter eggs—Fiction. 4. Easter—Fiction. 5. Dogs—Fiction.] I. Downer, Maggie, ill. II. Title. III. Series.
PZ7.H772Fpu 2006
1-59961-100-7 (reinforced library bound edition)

All Spotlight books are reinforced library binding and manufactured in the United States of America.

The BOBBSEY TWINS

Freddie and Flossie and the Easter Egg Hunt

by Laura Lee Hope

illustrated by Maggie Downer

Ready-to-Read

Aladdin

New York   London   Toronto   Sydney

Easter is here!

Freddie and Flossie
are on an Easter egg hunt.

Flossie looks under a flower.

No egg here.

Freddie looks beside a rock.

13

No egg here.

Flossie looks under a shrub.

No egg here.

Freddie looks in a tree.

Oops!

Where are the eggs?

See Snap.

Snap has the eggs!

29

Silly Snap!

Easter egg hunts
are for kids, not dogs!